ROBIN AND THE WHITE RABBIT

of related interest

The ASD and Me Picture Book
A Visual Guide to Understanding Challenges and
Strengths for Children on the Autism Spectrum
Joel Shaul
ISBN 978 1 78592 723 2
eISBN 978 1 78450 351 2

Lisa and the Lacemaker – The Graphic Novel
Kathy Hoopmann
Art and adaptation by Mike Medaglia
ISBN 978 1 78592 028 8
eISBN 978 1 78450 280 5

Our Brains Are Like Computers!
Exploring Social Skills and Social Cause and
Effect with Children on the Autism Spectrum
Joel Shaul
ISBN 978 1 84905 716 5
eISBN 978 1 78450 208 9

Tomas Loves…
A rhyming book about fun, friendship – and autism
Jude Welton
Illustrated by Jane Telford
ISBN 978 1 84905 544 4
eISBN 978 0 85700 969 2

What Is It Like to Be Me?
A Book About a Boy with Asperger's Syndrome
Alenka Klemenc
Illustrated by Urša Rožic
ISBN 978 1 84905 375 4
eISBN 978 0 85700 730 8

What Did You Say? What Do You Mean?
120 Illustrated Metaphor Cards, plus Booklet
with Information, Ideas and Instructions
Jude Welton
Illustrated by Jane Telford
ISBN 978 1 84310 924 2

ROBIN AND THE WHITE RABBIT

A story to help children with autism to talk about their feelings and join in

Emma Lindström and Åse Brunnström

Foreword by Tony Attwood
Illustrated by Emma Lindström

Jessica Kingsley Publishers
London and Philadelphia

First published in 2017
by Jessica Kingsley Publishers
73 Collier Street
London N1 9BE, UK
and
400 Market Street, Suite 400
Philadelphia, PA 19106, USA

www.jkp.com

Copyright © Emma Lindström 2017
Foreword copyright © Tony Attwood 2017

Library of Congress Cataloging in Publication Data
A CIP catalog record for this book is available from the Library of Congress

British Library Cataloguing in Publication Data
A CIP catalogue record for this book is available from the British Library

ISBN 978 1 78592 290 9
eISBN 978 1 78450 598 1

Printed and bound in China

Foreword

Traditional stories for young children were written to engage the child's interest and then succinctly educate the child in various aspects of morality and wisdom. This formula can be applied to educate children who have an Autism Spectrum Disorder to explore and express thoughts and feelings.

When asked, 'What are you thinking or feeling?', children with an ASD have great difficulty isolating one of the many emotions and thoughts swirling in their mind, and finding the precise words to accurately and eloquently explain those thoughts or feelings to another person. However, children may have a greater ability to visualize than verbalize thoughts and feelings – hence the creation of this picture book. The simple activity of using picture cards and symbols can help children express feelings and preferences. This will be extremely valuable information for parents and teachers, and will enable children to use a new form of communication.

The story also includes themes of friendship, encouragement and affection, and can be used to explain the world of autism to typical peers.

The messages and implications of this book could be written in many hefty volumes. The great value of this little story book is its brevity and eminent accessibility to adults and children alike.

Tony Attwood, The Minds and Hearts Clinic, Brisbane

It was just a normal day at school for Robin.

At break time, the grown-ups kept nagging Robin. "Hurry up and go outside with the other children." Go outside? To do what?

It's time to go outside now! The other children have already gone outside! Hurry up so you can play with the other children!

The other children were playing football, but Robin sat alone under a tree. Suddenly, a white rabbit appeared.

"Oh dear, Robin. Are you sitting all alone under the tree again? I think it's time I got my blue bag."

Words were tumbling around in Robin's head. Robin felt lots of different things at the same time. Robin wished that someone could understand these feelings.

meanwhile, the white rabbit had gone
back to its burrow and started to fill its
blue bag. Then the rabbit went to find
Robin, who was still sitting under the tree.

what is that sound?

What is going on?

Robin and the white rabbit looked at each other. At first they didn't say anything. Then the rabbit came closer and began to talk to Robin.

"Hello there!" said the rabbit.

"Hello," Robin replied.

"Why are you sitting here under the tree?"

"I don't know," said Robin.

"Hmm... Well, what do you like doing?"

"I don't know."

"Shall we find out what you like doing?"

"I don't know," said Robin, for the third time.

"I have brought my blue bag," said the rabbit.

"Is it OK if I show you some picture cards from it?"

"Yes, it is," replied Robin.

The rabbit pulled a pile of picture cards out of its blue bag.

"Have a look at this one. What does it feel like
when you are sitting under the tree?"

The rabbit drew a happy face. "Put the things you like doing under the happy face," the rabbit explained.

"If you don't know, you can put the picture card
in the middle," the rabbit explained as it drew a
red cross, "and you can put the things you don't
like under this red cross."

sit under tree

hide and seek

hopscotch

swing

ping pong

football

hockey

balance

sandpit

climb tree

"Do you like playing hide and seek?" asked the rabbit.
"I don't know," Robin replied.

"Do you like going on the swing?"
"I like to swing high, and I like the feeling I get in my stomach."

"Do you like playing hopscotch?"
"I don't like playing hopscotch, because my knee hurts when I jump."

"What about ping-pong?"
"I don't know because I have never tried it."

"What about playing football?"
"I don't like football. It hurts if I fall on the gravel."

"Do you like playing in the sand pit?"
"No, I don't. I don't like getting sand under my nails."

"What about going on the balance beam?"
"I don't know."

"Do you like playing hockey?"
"I think I would like it if I played it with a soft ball."

"What about climbing trees?"
"I **really** like that!" said Robin.

"OK, that's it! Now we know what you like, shall we find out **how much** you like these things? We'll rate each thing on a scale from 0 to 10. Ten is what you like best," explained the rabbit.

Robin picked up the "climb tree" card and put it at the top of the scale.

"It's fun to climb trees, but I don't want to do it all alone. Do you want to climb with me?" asked Robin.

10

climb tree

hockey

5

swing

sit under tree

0

The rabbit looked scared and replied, "Ooh...you see I'm a rabbit, and rabbits don't climb trees."

Robin smiled at the rabbit. "What if I give you a hug first, and then I'll help you climb the tree. Would that be OK?" asked Robin.

curious

important

happy

hopefu

brave

friendly

caring

elieved

peaceful

e   calm

joy
interested
satisfied

"How do you feel now?" asked the rabbit.

"I think I am happy and a bit curious," Robin replied.

"Oh! Can you see all the children?" asked the rabbit.

"Yes, one of them is waving to me!" Robin replied.

For those who have listened to the story of Robin and the white rabbit

Now you have listened to a story about me, Robin. I sat in the classroom and had a lot of feelings inside me. Then I sat under the tree and felt even more inside. I do not usually tell anyone what I feel, and I do not tell people what I like doing. The white rabbit asked me what I like doing, and I replied that I didn't know. But when the rabbit showed me the pictures of activities it was easier for me to express what I really like doing and what I don't like. I sorted the cards under three symbols when the rabbit and I sat under the tree. And then I graded them on a scale of 0 to 10. After that, the rabbit understood that what I like doing best is climbing trees!

If you are like me and find it hard to say what you like doing, then you can look for pictures of activities and do as I did in this story. When I sat up in the tree, I felt happy. I know I'm happy sometimes and sad sometimes, but there are more feelings than that. If you want, you can use the emotion words in the book to tell people what you feel. And you can look for more words for thoughts and feelings – there are a lot more to find.

Good luck, and a hug from me, Robin!

For those who have read the story

We have worked with feeling and emotion words, symbols and activity cards for a long time, both in our private lives and at work. We couldn't find a picture book that deals specifically with visual communication, so we decided to make this one. If, like us, you are already working with visual communication and need a picture book that involves the reader and the listener, then you have one here.

When the rabbit asked Robin, "What do you like doing?" Robin answered, "I don't know." Our experience tells us that this is a very common answer. After that, the rabbit tried to communicate visually to see what Robin likes doing best of all. Robin was sitting under the tree, but actually wanted to climb up the tree. How would the rabbit know that if it hadn't given Robin a chance to express it? Robin held a lot of feelings inside. But with help from the rabbit, Robin could express what makes Robin happy.

A first step to visualize thoughts and feelings is to write them down. If you like, you could use the emotion words from this book. You could use them to help children to express what they feel and also to see how many emotions there are to find.

To do what the rabbit does in the story, all you need is:

    Paper

    A black pen

    A red pen

    Pictures of activities (photos or drawings)

Then you can do exactly what the rabbit did in the book.

Greetings from Emma and Åse

The white rabbit has a website:
https://vitkanin.wordpress.com